If some people really see angels, where others see empty space, let them paint the angels.

JOHN RUSKIN

Copyright © 2005 by Jennifer Eachus

All rights reserved. No part of this book may be reproduced, transmitted, or stored in an information retrieval system in any form or by any means, graphic, electronic, or mechanical, including photocopying, taping, and recording, without prior written permission from the publisher.

First U.S. edition 2005

Library of Congress Cataloging-in-Publication Data is available.

Library of Congress Catalog Card Number 2005045381

ISBN 0-7636-2953-7

2 4 6 8 10 9 7 5 3 1

Printed in China

This book was typeset in Eva Antiqua.
The illustrations were done in colored pencil.

Candlewick Press
2067 Massachusetts Avenue
Cambridge, Massachusetts 02140

visit us at www.candlewick.com

ANGEL
A TALE OF WONDER

Jennifer Eachus

CANDLEWICK PRESS
CAMBRIDGE, MASSACHUSETTS

In a corner of her garden,
Lara found a soft white feather
fallen to the earth.
"Look," she said. "A feather
from an angel."

Next she found a scrap of cloth hanging from a branch. Gold threads glistened in the sun. It's from the angel's dress, she thought.

In the morning sunshine,

beside the big old tree,

Lara saw a fox crossing

the field.

And suddenly the angel

was there!

"Will you tell me something,
Lara?" the angel asked.
Lara nodded.
"Will you tell me what
you know about wonder?"
Lara kept silent.
"Go now and find the answer."

"What is wonder?" Lara asked her father.
"Wonder," he said, "is sitting by the river
on a summer evening, watching fish
among the weeds."

"What is wonder?" Lara asked her mother.
"Wonder," her mother said, "is when
the thrush sings so sweetly from the
tree, you forget the time of day."

"What is wonder?" Lara asked her brother.
"Shooting stars are wonderful," her brother said.
"They whiz across the sky so fast that if you
blink for just one second, they're gone."

Lara ran to tell the angel what
she had found out about wonder—
about fish, the thrush, and shooting stars.

The angel listened carefully.
"Those things are wonderful, it's true."
she said. "But please, Lara, tell me
something wonderful of your own."

It had all been wonderful, Lara
thought—the feather and the scrap of
cloth and the fox under the big old tree.
But the angel was most wonderful of all.

"Everything is wonderful,"
Lara said. "You make the
whole world wonderful.
You are my angel, and you
are most wonderful of all."

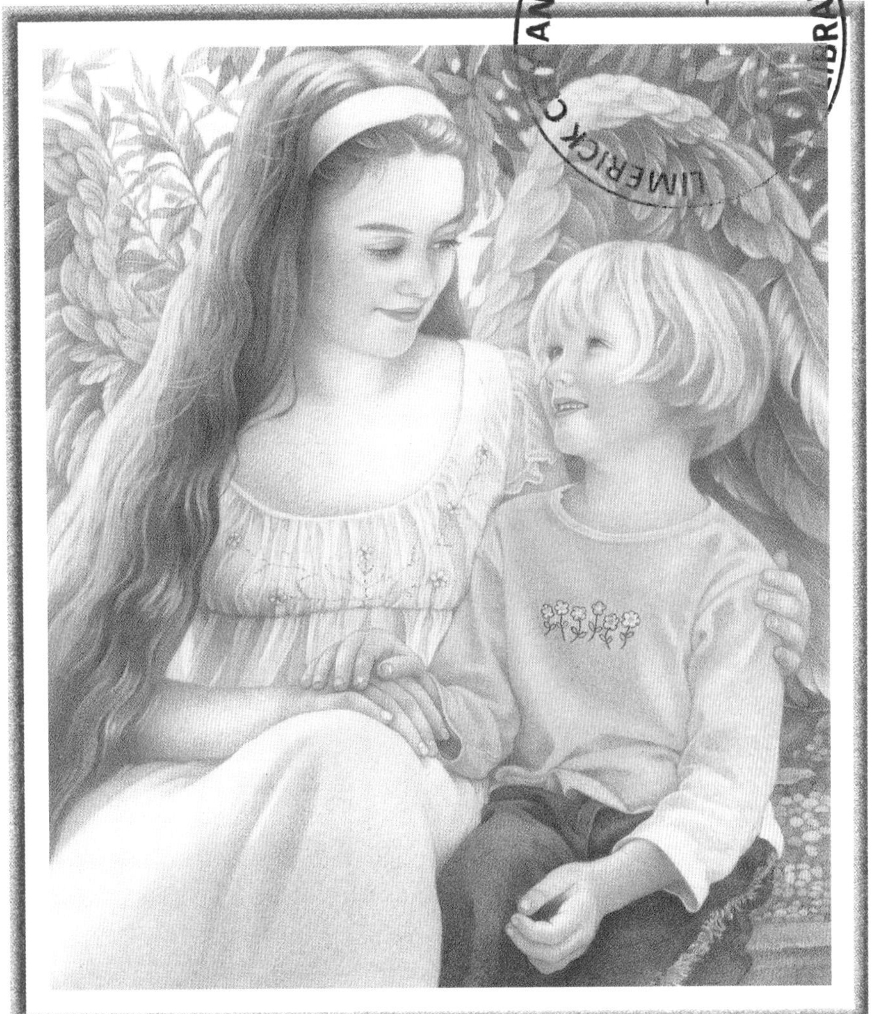

The angel smiled.

She spread her feathered wings

until they filled the garden.

"Thank you, Lara," she said . . .

And suddenly

the angel was gone.

It was still morning in

Lara's garden.

The sun shone through

the big old tree.

And far away,

to someone else,

a soft white feather came

falling from the sky.